Integrity For the Mission

Barry Barnes

CONTENTS

UNTO HIM

Lord Jesus, I just want to open with my gratefulness towards You. You stated in Jeremiah 1:5, "Before I (You, Lord) formed you (me, Barry) in the womb I (You, Lord) knew you (me, Barry), before you (me, Barry) were born I (You, Lord) set you (me, Barry) apart; I (You, Lord) appointed you (me, Barry) as a prophet to the nations."

It was not until when I turned 16 years old, I found out about Your trust. So, I humbly gave my life to you completely. Nevertheless, I did not understand this fact until later in my life as I became a student of your Word and patterned my lifestyle around your Word. From where I came from to now, as I sit here, writing a book regarding your principles to serve the men and women of God is tremendous and unbelievable.

Only You could have prepared this path, and I thank You forever and ever. Thank You, Father!

ACKNOWLEDGEMENTS

Traditionally, it is stated to save 'the best for last.' Well, I'm a proud mode breaker, and I will start with my best acknowledgement on earth, which is my wife - Latia Barnes.

Thank you, LaTia for allowing me to help you in our algebra class in the tenth grade. Thank you for allowing me to walk you to class. Most importantly, thank you for introducing me to Christ and, years later, saying yes to my hand in marriage. Thank you for seeing Christ working with me long before I did because I was a class clown. I thank you for the four boys you were willing to bear for us, with God's purposes in the forefront. I would not be where I am now - I still with a long way to go. After 20-plus years, I'm looking forward to where we will continue to advance together. I acknowledge you as the best first because that is where you belong - at first.

Thank you, Deacon William Brown, for recognizing me in my youth to potentially walk with the man of God. You taught me all I know about serving the man of God and encouraged me to be greater in this lifestyle. To Apostle David Brown, thank you for laying the foundation of what a leader is to be, teaching the Word of God with simplicity and grace, and being bold for Christ only.

Thank you, George Davis, for teaching me how to read and understand the Word for myself and making me the student of God's Word I am today. Sitting at your feet and learning from you helped change my life.

Dr. Bishop Art Robinson, of Bring It To Life Ministries, thank you for pushing me to levels I thought it would be impossible to reach. And thanks to my uncle, the late James Gatling, and a host of situations helped to mold me to the man of God I am today.

Okay, time to end these acknowledgements. I have a book to write!

INTEGRITY FOR THE MISSION

Let's talk about the principles of armor bearing or serving. Through this text, armor bearer will be referenced as a role, calling, servanthood, watchman, or adjutant. Still, the walk of being an armor bearer is a lifestyle.

Ezekiel 3:17

17 "Son of man, I have made you a watchman for the house of Israel. Whenever you hear a word from my mouth, you shall give them warning from me.

Being an armor bearer it is definitely more of a lifestyle than just taking on a role. It should never be a plug-and-play situation. You have to take the lifestyle of servanthood very seriously, and it is a conduct that you don't take lightly.

Isaiah 62:6

On your walls, O Jerusalem, I have set watchmen; all the day and all the night they shall never be silent. You who put the Lord in remembrance, take no rest,

Sometimes, you'll find yourself in situations where you can probably make some people mad or offended with the way you handle the man and woman of God, but that's alright because you're doing your job.

Walking in the lifestyle of being an armor bearer is a calling that you definitely have to take seriously. It's a critical assignment that frees up the man and woman of God so they can have the liberty to pursue and accomplish the mission of being a restoration to God's people.

An armor bearer is like a watchman. In servanthood, we are watchmen.

A watchman's duty, especially during biblical times, is always to anticipate any possible danger. Anything can happen, especially during biblical times. Clearly, there are things that we can reflect on today in the spirit and the natural in terms of walking in the lifestyle of an armor bearer.

Ezekiel 33:1-5

1 The word of the Lord came to me:

2 "Son of man, speak to your people and say to them, If I bring the sword upon a land, and the people of the land take a man from among them, and make him their watchman,

3 and if he sees the sword coming upon the land and blows the trumpet and warns the people,

4 Then if anyone who hears the sound of the trumpet does not take warning, and the sword comes and takes him away, his blood shall be upon his own head.

5 He heard the sound of the trumpet and did not take warning; his blood shall be upon himself. But if he had taken warning, he would have saved his life.

We get into more detail later. But the watchman's job is to always, always anticipate anything to go wrong, any danger. Now, no individual in this position wishes for some time to transpire. It is a fact that servicing at this type of capacity acquires no foolishness. A watchman shares his perspective and advice with his or her pastor and then responds according to the leader's wishes. Apparently, it will take some time before you can be in a position where you can give your man or woman of God some sound advice. Nevertheless, an armor bearer's duty is to execute the needs of the man or woman of God.

CHAPTER 1
SIT, SHUT UP AND
LEARN THE HOUSE

Acts 20:28

Pay careful attention to yourselves and to all the flock, in which the Holy Spirit has made you overseers, to care for the church of God, which he obtained with his own blood.

Being a servant, you may experience different and unique situations and demands. One situation in particular is serving under another ministry. Meaning you came from one ministry with the idea of believing you can do the same exact things at the new fellowship as a servant.

That is not always the case. If you leave from one city to go into another one, you don't know how the atmosphere is in that area. You have to learn about the city, find where the markets are, the places of entertainment, show yourself friendly to neighbors, etc. Sometimes, you have to get lost in order to not make the same mistake again.

You can not come into your new city expecting the same traffic patterns, believing the people are the same, and taking the new findings for granted.

You just can't come into anyone's surroundings believing you can serve in the same capacity and execute the same duties at the new church home.

Many have found that the former approach will not always apply because each situation is different and unique. That is why it is important that we sit and learn about the house and the man or woman of God. It is best to honestly shut up and learn the ministry before you make yourself available to serve.

Now, being an armor bearer is a different call of duty.

1 Peter 4:10-11

10 As each has received a gift, use it to serve one another, as good stewards of God's varied grace:

11 Whoever speaks, as one who speaks oracles of God; whoever serves, as one who serves by the strength that God supplies—in order that in everything God may be glorified through Jesus

Christ. To him belong glory and dominion forever and ever. Amen.

An armor bearer has to be sensitive to the man or woman of God's needs and wants.

Hebrews 13:17

Obey your leaders and submit to them, for they are keeping watch over your souls, as those who will have to give an account. Let them do this with joy and not with groaning, for that would be of no advantage to you.

An armor bearer has to make sure that they are in a situation where they are in tune, almost to the point where they are the man or woman of God's shadow. Before a candidate accepts the job of serving, in whatever capacity it may be, a servant has to make sure that they are in sync with the man or woman of God. The only way to do so is by sitting and learning the house, and do not be so anxious.

Be mindful of those who are eager to serve, especially close to the man or woman of God. Where there is eagerness, there are potential agendas. There is nothing wrong with having a desire to serve the man or woman of God.

Nevertheless, forcing the issue without respecting the house and those in positions of authority is a clear indication that the individual has an agenda that is unbecoming of the Lord.

A quick understanding of an individual's motive is simple. If he or she approaches servanthood in the ministry with the outright position of voicing the task can be 'better than' the procedure that is in place; they need to sit or put in their place. These individuals can not help themselves. They easily expose themselves immediately due to being pushy and aggressive. When he or she believes they have someone's ear in the newfound ministry, they will eagerly voice their opinion in a short matter of time.

Now, let's say the potential servant is correct as he or she understands protocol recognizing some procedures may be off a bit. If he or she has an impulse to serve properly, they will sit, learn the house, learn the flow of that particular ministry and stay humble. When the opportunity presents itself, one must have the appropriate spirit and still be willing to understand the process. When the liberty is given to express a change in the procedures, the information will be received well, and credibility will be established.

So, when it's time to move forward, and you are chosen to step into a certain area of servanthood, you will feel comfortable knowing that you can execute the duties because you appropriately took the time to understand the house and respect all the individuals in place.

CHAPTER 2
TRUE (POSITIVE) ATTRIBUTES, FALSE (NEGATIVE) ATTRIBUTES

Now, the armor bearer should possess other attributes, like faithfulness, knowing who they are (personality), and being confident. They have to be a man and woman of prayer. The armor bearer has to be a person of integrity. Better yet, have integrity for the mission.

POSITIVE ATTITUDE

The armor bearer must remain integral in all situations so the man or woman of God can have trustworthiness in them. Trustworthiness is not just established while being with the man or woman of God, but when the armor-bearer is at the gas station, walking around in a local grocery market, at work, and at home.

2 Peter 1:5-9

5 For this very reason, make every effort to supplement your faith with virtue, and virtue with knowledge,

6 and knowledge with self-control, and self-control with steadfastness, and steadfastness with godliness,

7 and godliness with brotherly affection, and brotherly affection with love.

8 For if these qualities are yours and are increasing, they keep you from being ineffective or unfruitful in the knowledge of our Lord Jesus Christ.

9 For whoever lacks these qualities is so nearsighted that he is blind, having forgotten that he was cleansed from his former sins.

Scenario: the armor bearer is not at the church and they are at a gas station. At the gas station during the winter months, they are trying to pump the gas, and all of a sudden, the armor bearer gets mad that the clip holder in the gas pump handle will not stay locked. They begin to display actions and behaviors unbecoming of the calling.

The armor bearer is at the local grocer. They are in a line, and the person in front of them is taking a long time. The individual may have an assistance card. The armor bearer begins to voice publicly,

"Ugh. God. Come on, man. What's taking so long?" As a servant of God, no one should easily blow their gasket.

Anything, both small or great, that is done inappropriately outside the church can tarnish a ministry, especially when someone responds in a negative way.

You never know who is watching! Remember, being an armor bearer is a lifestyle!

An armor bearer is at their place of work talking about things they should not be discussing or interacting with. Their co-workers know the church they go to. They know who you are affiliated with. Then, the integrity of the church and the leadership will take a hit because of the way the armor bearer carries themselves outside the ministry.

Don't compromise the integrity of the church or the leadership of the house and then expect to be effective for the man or woman of God.

The armor bearer or servant must remain positive by realizing and appreciating the importance of his or her calling to, number one, serve God first. Then, the man or woman of God. Their commitment first is always to the Lord. When an armor bearer makes their commitment to the Lord that they are going to help establish His kingdom on the earth, with their relationship with Christ, the directive and focus will be easier.

2 Timothy 2:15

Do your best to present yourself to God as one approved, a worker who has no need to be ashamed, rightly handling the word of truth.

If you are "called" by God to a particular ministry and you are called upon to serve in a certain capacity, do so. However, it's always God first because the Lord is not going to allow just anybody to be with His mouthpiece. It's not an assignment that anybody can execute. In essence, you definitely want to make sure that your commitment is to Christ first, then the ministry, and, if the Lord sees fit, your commitment to the man or woman of God who would allow you the opportunity to serve them as their armor bearer.

HAVING AN APPROPRIATE RELATIONSHIP

The armor bearer will be in an intimate space with the man or woman of God. Oftentimes, as the armor bearer, they will be in situations where the man or woman of God will be vulnerable, especially mentally. The last thing the man or woman of God needs is to be mishandled.

It is imperative for the armor bearer to be careful and aware of the privacy that is bestowed onto them by the man or woman of God due to the intimacy, where they are close to them in ways that nobody else is. Outside of their spouse, if married, there is personal information that will be exposed to the armor bearer by the man or woman of God that no one from the congregation or another ministry should ever know about.

Ezekiel 3:16-19

16 And at the end of seven days, the word of the Lord came to me:

17 "Son of man, I have made you a watchman for the house of Israel. Whenever you hear a word from my mouth, you shall give them warning from me.

18 If I say to the wicked, 'You shall surely die,' and you give him no warning, nor speak to warn the wicked from his wicked way, in order to save his life, that wicked person shall die for his iniquity, but his blood I will require at your hand.

19 But if you warn the wicked, and he does not turn from his wickedness, or from his wicked way, he shall die for his iniquity, but you will have delivered your soul.

The adjutant is another word for an armor bearer or a watchman. An armor bearer must make sure that in every way possible, their leader, the man or woman of God, feels comfortable knowing that they will be secured, handled with respect, and can deliver God's Word with no distractions. That is the first thing the adjutant must institute right off the bat, that the man or woman of God knows that they can have confidence in them. The last thing the man or woman of God needs to stress about is the competency of their adjutant.

<u>*Hebrews 13:17*</u>

Obey your leaders and submit to them, for they are keeping watch over your souls, as those who will have to give an account. Let them do this with joy and not with groaning, for that would be of no advantage to you.

Clearly, no one is perfect, including the man or woman of God and the armor bearer. In rare circumstances, misunderstandings and conflicts can easily come about between a pastor and his or her adjutant. The armor bearer must keep his or her interaction with the man or woman of God appropriate and honest. The relationship between the armor bearer and the man or woman of God must be appropriately aligned because, once the moment something is out of order or misunderstood, the relationship between them can be fractured.

To avoid any mishandling and inappropriate behavior, the attention of service must be done unto the Lord and no one else, including the man or woman of God.

<u>*Colossians 3:23-25*</u>

23 Whatever you do, work heartily, as for the Lord and not for men,

24 knowing that from the Lord you will receive the inheritance as your reward. You are serving the Lord Christ.

25 For the wrongdoer will be paid back for the wrong he has done, and there is no partiality.

NEGATIVE ATTITUDES AND MOTIVES

Romans 2:8

But for those who are self-seeking and do not obey the truth, but obey unrighteousness, there will be wrath and fury.

For the 'Granddaddy' of them all, that good-old pompous, self-seeking spirit.

If an individual can not handle being ignored, is unappreciative, does not like being overlooked, has to be in control, is critical about every little thing, is deceptive, prideful, competitive in a negative way, or does not respect themselves, servicing the man or woman of God at the capacity of an armor bearer is not for them.

Apparently, the armor-bearers must disown themselves or get out of their own way. In servanthood, it is not an on-and-off switch. It is a lifestyle! Everything that we do, especially as believers, constitutes our lifestyle as we must walk and live in God's obedience because people, or better yet, the world, are watching. And most importantly, the Lord is watching.

Now, to avoid these dangerous attitudes, the adjutant must be teachable, an excellent communicator, and at the same time, follow directives. The adjutants must express themselves in a way of love and kindness. Don't be too boastful and too aggressive. A leader does not want someone to just push him or her around or try to take them over. It's a slippery slope in how the adjutant handles the man or woman of God. The man or woman of God must be treated carefully. Always stay teachable, tentative, and communicative.

What someone does behind closed doors, how they handle themselves on social media, and how they handle themselves in public with their friends or family is critical to the calling of an armor bearer. Without a doubt, this applies to every believer, however, for an armor bearer, it is equally as critical as a leader due to the mantle of responsibility they carry for Christ.

What is done in silence is going to eventually, somehow, someway, come out, or it's going to interfere with servanthood. What we do in silence counts. Can you be quiet? An armor bearer should never use the privilege or opportunity in private with the man or woman of God to always express your opinion. If you feel that you can not be quiet and always believe you have to say something, the walk of an armor bearer is not suited for that individual.

Jeremiah 9:23-24

Thus says the LORD: "Let not the wise man boast in his wisdom, let not the mighty man boast in his might, let not the rich man boast in his riches, but let him who boasts boast in this, that he understands and knows me, that I am the LORD who practices steadfast love, justice, and righteousness in the earth. For in these things I delight, declares the LORD."

Are you a glory seeker? Do you seek opportunities to bang your chest about being a leader's armor bearer? You are not the one! Go sit yourself down! You're not the one. If you're seeking that glory just to have a name, you are not the one to cover a leader.

Do you feel needy? Do you need to feel validated by man? Do you have to do something to show value to yourself? If you're a needy person, you cannot cover the man or woman of God, you cannot. Are you comfortable? Or better yet, are you confident in yourself? If you have confidence in yourself, you know what you are supposed to do to fulfill your duties. If you are down on yourself and you are always second-guessing, you lack the confidence needed, and you cannot serve the man and woman of God.

You have to walk in the authority God has given you, but not in a conceited way. The chosen individual has to know that if something was to go down and they have to step in to provide a word of comfort, they have to be confident to do so. If you often question yourself, nervous and scared, you cannot serve the man and woman of God in the capacity of the armor-bearer.

CHAPTER 3
SERVICING EXPECTATIONS

Adjutants often act as protectors, prayer warriors, a watchmen over their leader at all times.

Depending on the relationship, an adjutant should communicate with their man or woman of God consistently. It is key for the armor bearer to be locked in. The armor bearer should spiritually cover their man or woman in prayer with consistency, as prayer is imperative. The armor bearer must have their leader's back, not just in front of the people, but in private. The majority of the work is actually when the armor-bearer is apart from their man or woman of God, not only to just show face in public.

The armor bearer should be discerning to the needs of their man or woman of God. Catering is probably too strong; however, attending to the man or woman of God is important for the sake of an extended support system. Remember, leaders are people, and like all individuals, there's so much that they go through privately as well. Before it's time for them to preach or teach, the man or woman of God could be going through stuff at home, at the workplace, socially, health, etc. Without direct communication, the only way to be in tune with the man or woman of God is by prayer.

When the man or woman of God is spending time with the Lord in preparation for the word, there are so many challenges the enemy will present to them. And the last thing the man or woman of God needs, when it's time for them to go out to minister, is to deal with someone who does not know what they are doing and does not have things in order. That's the last thing the man or woman of God needs to deal with before they go out in front of the people.

This is essential as well: can you keep your mouth off the man or woman of God? The professional relationship between an armor bearer and the man or woman of God is a borderline intimate relationship right next to the spouse. There will be conversations, situations, and other personal manners that will be revealed that other people should not know about. Can you keep your mouth off of it? If you are a gossiper, can not control your tongue, or do not value concealment, you absolutely can not walk with the man or woman of God.

CHAPTER 4
QUALIFICATIONS

There is no educational requirement to be an armor bearer. Simply put, a man or woman of God has to like the selected individual. Now, some ministries may want their adjutant to have a bachelor's or a master's degree or some certification. It is whatever preference the man or woman of God has. For the most part, it really comes down to how the man or woman of God views the individual. If they like them on a personal level and feel confident that the person of interest is going to cover them unto the Lord is one of the normal qualifications.

Another thing a man or woman of God will look at, as far as doctrine, the person of interest shares the same views according to God's word. These are the things that a leader would look for. Is the person of interest liked? Do they have a relationship with Christ, and is it reflected in their lifestyle? Do they know the Word of God? What is their commitment to the house and the kingdom of God? Are they ministry-minded?

Ministry-minded means that the man or woman of God needs to make sure that his or her armor bearer knows and understands the mission of the house and will not do anything to discredit the ministry. Do they have the heart for God's people? Most importantly, always being ministry-minded means when you heed the 'call,' as an example for Christ, your sole duty is to help establish His kingdom of earth.

An armor bearer has to have the ability to stand in place and be in the gap for the man and woman of God. That basically means they have to be an intercessor, have to be a praying man or woman of God. Having to be a praying man or woman of God, they must be willing to intercept spiritual, mental, physical, and sometimes financial problems for your leader. There are things that an armor bearer has to take on and be ready for.

At the end of the day, the man or woman of God is going to be the one who will help teach the armor-bearer how to handle them. The last thing the man or woman of God wants is an unprepared covering to be lost and confused, which can lead to an embarrassing situation. How the man or woman of

God wants to be handled, the armor bearer must do it according to the needs of the leader because they know the temperament they must be in before standing in front of the people.

Generally speaking, it is ultimately the decision of the man or woman of God. It is always ideal to have a female with a female and have a male assigned to a male because perception is paramount.

If the man of God appoints a woman as his adjutant, or vice versa, nothing could be going on or wrong. She's doing her job as a married or single woman. The man of God could be married or single, and again, there's nothing inappropriate happening between them. However, in terms of perception, by nature, the first thing that goes through the mind of many individuals is, 'Oh, they are sleeping together, or there's something about that that doesn't sit right.'

Ephesians 4:27

27 and give no opportunity to the devil.

1 Thessalonians 5:22

22 Abstain from every form of evil.

So far as perception is concerned, it is best to have a male with a male and a female with a female because, especially in the ministry, we are dealing with individuals with fragile minds. We are dealing with people who are broken and facing critical situations and as soon as they attend a church service and witness such an arrangement, no telling what they will comprehend or interpret.

Ephesians 4:12

To equip the saints for the work of ministry, for building up the body of Christ.

CHAPTER 5
HOME SUPPORT

There has to be an agreement within the household of the armor-bearer. If the armor bearer has a family, all parties in the household have to be in agreement and on one accord. Everyone, especially if they are married. Ideally, most leaders will look for someone who is single because that person can solely focus on the man and woman of God. However, the armor bearer, whether a husband or wife, spouse and everyone in the house has to be in agreement, recognizes the calling and duties that apply to serving the man or woman of God.

The schedule for the day of serving, especially when there is an additional service outside the normal day of worship, must be detailed to the spouse. If the household has a child or children, the order has to be in place for them. Is there food in the refrigerator? Does the spouse have money for an emergency? Does the family have to change their plans due to covering the man or woman of God? Is the spouse happy about this? Everyone has to be on the same page. If everyone is on the same page, the armor bearer can go and serve freely with a clear conscience.

An armor bearer can not serve a man or woman of God when their power is off. Who will be able to think straight when their family has no power? Situations and circumstances will always surface. Nevertheless, the home has to be in order because, if the house is not in order, focusing on the man or woman of God could be trying. Clearly, the household must be in sync, not just for the armor bearer, but for the man or woman of God as they will ultimately benefit as they flow spiritually with a focused covering.

CHAPTER 6
'THE SIX ACCOUNTABILITIES'

Now, there is a question that you have to ask yourselves: why do you want to serve? Why do you want to serve in a certain capacity? Why do you want to be an armor-bearer? You have to ask yourself the question, "Why do I want to serve at this magnitude?"

There are several requirements a potential armor-bearer needs to account for before they are considered the privilege of this call. Nevertheless, these six accountabilities are often either overlooked or not given much thought in terms of public duties for the man or woman of God.

1. Heart To Serve

Ephesians 6:7

Serve wholeheartedly, as if you were serving the Lord, not people.

When it comes to serving, serving is something that cannot be taught. It's just something that has to be in you. In sports, it is stated, "You can't teach height. A person can not be taught how to grow in length." In terms of serving, an individual can't teach someone to serve. Serving is not just an action because anyone can be instructed what to do. Nevertheless, serving it is a matter of the heart. The desire to serve is an action of the heart and passion, and that can not be taught.

If you want more for yourself, whether it's in ministry, whether it's in your career, or to be a better parent, servanthood is the doorway to it. Serving is the doorway to whatever you want. The humbling of the heart makes serving effective. Serving puts you in a vulnerable position. The Lord recognizes that, and He'll be willing to allow you to move into greatness because you are willing to sacrifice your name, your pride, your knees, your hands, your nails, and whatever else, and more.

If you want to be elevated in ministry, you have the heart of a servant. And to go higher, you must learn how to serve the man or woman of God with the right heart and spirit. If you have to start off cleaning toilets, you have to do that. If you have to start off cleaning the church, you have to do that. If you have to take open rebuke, you have to take it, take it, and take it without focusing on other individuals.

2. Be In Place

It must be understood that serving the man and woman of God is not a job. It's a privilege. It's an honor. So, if an individual is walking in the calling of the armor bearer, when the man or woman of God calls, they have to go.

There are several attributes that constitute a man or woman of God as a great leader. In terms of the armor bearer, a great leader will never place them in a situation where it could jeopardize their family. If a matter occurs and after a man or woman of God has exhausted all their options if they have to call for the armor bearer, they must assist.

3. Preparedness

For starters, no man or woman of God should pick up their armor bearer from their residence or meeting place. An armor bearer has to be at a place to handle the needs of their man or woman of God, which includes having a valid driver's license. Does the president of the United States have to drive themselves around for anything, especially if they have to make an appearance? This aggressive comparison is necessary because this nation's highest official, who is recognized throughout the world, garners this attention. Surely, God's man or woman who is representing Him as His mouthpiece should be allotted this privilege.

When it's time to get the man and woman of God from their location, transportation needs to be cleaned, gassed up, have the atmosphere conducive for the spirit, and refreshments should be either inside the vehicle or available. The man or woman of God will always be fresh, energized, and later, replenished.

The man or woman of God goes through all kinds of warfare because the Word they have to bring forth is going to be seasoned. They may be going through stuff with the family, the job (if the man or woman of God works), their stockings have a run in it, suits probably not as clean as they want them to be, and so forth. All these obstacles and situations are going on in their mind, and the last thing they need is an adjutant, an armor-bearer who does not know what they're doing and doesn't have anything in place properly. The negligence of an armor bearer is an unnecessary obstacle that a man or woman should not have to hurdle before they go in front of the people.

When the man or woman of God gets inside the vehicle, and they recognize their physical needs to replenish are met before and after they complete their assignment, they will be at ease. The satisfaction and gratitude go a long way, and the man or woman of God will greatly appreciate it because it demonstrates care and appreciation for God's gift to the body of Christ. When they return home or to their place of recovery, the man or woman of God will be energized to spend time with their spouse, family, or whatever they desire to do personally for themselves.

4. *Prep financially*

As the armor-bearer, an individual should always be aware of their man or woman of God's scheduled assignments to preach. The man or woman of God should notify their armor-bearer weeks in advance. Suppose the armor bearer does not have extra money due to salary month expenses because of family or circumstances. There's nothing wrong with that situation. However, if the armor bearer knows weeks in advance that their man or woman of God is going out for an assignment, funds need to be allocated for that occasion. While on an assignment, an issue may occur; the man or woman of God may need or want something. Items need to be in place, and, which is extremely important, when it's time to give an offering, the adjutant should be prepared to give. When the believers get up to give, and the armor bearer does not move because they do not have any money, their actions can be labeled as an embarrassment to their leader.

An armor bearer, who is sitting on the pulpit covering their man or woman of God, should never come empty-handed because they are representing the church and the man or woman of God. Armor bearer, never be empty-handed. Always be prepared to give because the pastor of that church and other leaders are watching because the armor bearer is a reflection of their leader.

It is important to allocate funds. Put money aside because the armor bearer represents their leader, church and they have to be ready.

5. *Looking The Part*

The armor bearer's physical appearance has to be on point and look appropriate. Not smelling funky, being well groomed, having a haircut, and everything in place. The armor bearer has to always be presentable, not flashy. The armor bearer must always present well but, at the same time, be forgotten.

For example: If the man of God is wearing a black suit, the armor-bearer cannot wear a lime green suit or some red shoes because they would be a distraction. The only thing the people are going to remember and say, 'Did you see what the armor bearer had on? A lime green suit?' All their attention should be on what the Lord is saying through the man of God, however, the people would be captivated by the lime green suit looking like a fool and the people would potentially miss God.

An armor bearer has to mirror their man or woman of God as they are a reflection of them.

When the woman of God is called for an assignment, and she's wearing blue, her adjutant must mirror her. The adjutant should not wear neon shoes, bright makeup all caked up with crazy eye shadows, and have a standout hairstyle overshadowing the woman of God. Have on the right size bra to keep them 'girls up.' If the woman of God keeps her hair simple, her armor bearer needs to do the same.

Whether the armor bearer shows out or presents themselves sloppy, all the attention will shift right over to them, which could lead to an embarrassing situation. Due to the carnality of the people, the whole time, while the man or woman of God is bringing forth the Word of God from the pulpit, they could be distracted by the outward appearance of the armor-bearer. Always look presentable, but at the same time, forgotten.

In terms of the man or woman God, the armor bearer must make sure their leader stands out appropriately and looks sharp from head to toe. Make sure there are no wrinkles, lint, dirt, etc.

Have a lint roller or brush, an emergency sewing kit, aspirin, hair glue, or any necessity to make sure the man or woman God's appearance will never come into question.

Now, this situation rarely happens, and if a trusting relationship is established, if the man or woman of God is dressed inappropriately - with grace - expresses the need for them to change. The man of God should be dressed like a man of God, not a gigolo or feminine. The woman of God should be dressed like ' a woman' of God, not provocative, exposing all her curves with her cleavage out and panty line showing.

Honesty, if the woman of God is dressed that way, most men will be attracted to what they see and not to what the Lord is saying. An armor bearer must help keep their man or woman of God looking respectful as well. The man and woman of God have only one job to execute. There's only one thing on their mind: bring forth the Word of God.

It is wise for an armor bearer not to wear any colognes or perfumes. From the man or woman of God to other individuals who may come into contact with an armor bearer, a person may be allergic to a particular scent or smell that is worn. Just be clean. To be safe or use wisdom, do not wear any colognes or perfumes at all because it is unknown what kind of reaction someone may receive.

6. Being The Part

No matter the size or shape of the servant, an armor bearer must be physically fit and in shape. An armor bearer has to be physically fit to fully occupy this assignment because the demands of being focused, attentive, and alert will take a physical toll on the body, especially if there are multiple services spanning a couple of days. The assignment of an armor bearer is unpredictable. There is no indication of how the spirit is going to move or how the Lord is going to use the man or woman of God.

Let's be clear: the service is not for the armor-bearer to enjoy and have church as usual. Prior to either getting to church to serve or meeting with the man or woman of God, the armor bearer should have had their time with the Lord and be in a place of worship because when it is time to cover their leader, they are on duty.

When the man or woman of God is on assignment, it is not the time for the armor bearer to be engrossed with the meet and greet with the other leaders and officials, even if there's familiarity. When service starts, it is not time for the armor bearer to get into praise and worship mode. The duty is for the armor bearer to be on guard, watching over their man or woman of God. Eyes are always open, even in prayer. If the assignment is located at a known ministry or not, the armor bearer must always be on guard. If there's seating for the armor bearer, he or she needs to sit at the edge of the chair in a responsive position so they can react quickly if needed.

As a media member with the Baltimore Ravens in 2012, I had the privilege to join the team at the White House. At the White House, which is both scary and breathtaking, I witnessed how the Secret Service was everywhere but not seen. Protecting the president of the United States is an unpredictable assignment whether it's at a place of familiarity, the White House, or not, a secret service agent must always be on guard. The armor bearer's mentality of covering the man or woman of God should mirror the same approach as a secret service agent because of the importance of the assignment.

For the armor bearer, there is no shouting, clapping, jumping, running, laughing, dancing, singing, or anything like a spectator of the service. The duty of the armor bearer is to cover and guard the anointing of the man or woman of God both spiritually and physically because anything can happen at any time and anywhere. Always remember the armor bearer is not there for the service. They are there solely for the man or woman of God. Their eyes are on them, the whole time, and at the same time, being alert and monitoring their surroundings.

Just because the man or woman of God fellowshipped at a particular church for a number of years and nothing ever jumped off, the armor bearer must stay alert. This is displaying the integrity of the assignment.

Several years ago, Overseer Rose Robinson had an assignment to preach at a familiar fellowship in downtown Baltimore. She was preaching the word, and then all of a sudden, a gentleman stepped into the aisle and started walking down slowly towards her. I stepped down from the pulpit and stood at the edge step. He got closer and closer. And while the Overseer Rose was preaching, the gentleman was trying to get to her. I came from the edge of the step and cut the gentleman off at the front altar, pushed him in the chest, and moved him back.

I stood there for the remainder of the service to let him know that he was not getting near her, all the while, the service was not interrupted. As soon as Overseer finished her assignment, I quickly escorted her to the vehicle. It does not matter if the spirit or emotions are high in the service; the armor bearer has to stand at attention and be alert because anything can happen. Be attentive spiritually and physically.

Clearly, the assignment of the armor bearer is not only spiritual but it's physical. Due to the assignment demands, the armor bearer must be physically fit and in shape because the duties can wear an individual down. After the man and woman of God's assignment are over, they are exhausted from giving the word and bringing restoration to God's people. They don't need their armor bearer walking sluggishly with them. The armor bearer needs to be upright, focused, tentative and alert more than they were at the beginning of service, even if the adjutant had to stand all service due to lack of seating or placement. Thus the reason to be physically fit and in shape, despite their size and shape. When the armor-bearer gets to their place of rest, then they can pass out.

There's a standard of excellence that needs to be reflected. The man or woman of God can not be handled in any kind of way. It is the duty of armor bearers to set the tone of their man or woman of God to be handled and treated. Not everyone and anyone can just walk up on the man or woman of God. While reading the room and understanding the atmosphere, there are times when an armor bearer has to run interference between their leader and other individuals. Be firm but gentle. There is a standard of excellence and respect that must be set, and that starts with the armor-bearer.

Can an armor bearer be effective and not be noticed? Can an armor bearer's silence speak louder than words? An armor bearer should not be talking to the man or woman of God en route to the service. The one-on-one quiet time with the man or woman of God is not the time to fulfill a personal motive. They should not. The only time it is appropriate for the armor bearer to talk to their man or woman of God, if they are together en route to an assignment is when they are engaged in a conversation with the man or woman of God. And if the armor bearer is engaged in a conversation, do not keep the leisure going. The leaders have to put themselves in the proper spirit to bring forth God's word. The armor bearer is not to entertain but to serve.

Depending on the relationship between the armor bearer and their leader, the duty can span to other assignments away from church. The duty of an armor bearer is to make sure that the man or woman of God is always covered, especially when it's time for them to bring forth the word.

And when it's time to get the man or woman of God out of the service, it's not like they don't want to talk to the people, but they physically don't have the energy to engage the people fully like they want to. The man or woman of God is vulnerable at this point. It's the armor bearer's job to get them to their place of safety in order to get them home.

Now, the man or woman of God is at a familiar church, surrounded by friends and acquaintances. The armor bearer may know the people as well. Service may be over. However, It's still not a time to greet and talk to those people because the armor bearer is on duty. It's not a time to play patty cake and try to catch up. Be nice and cordial, but for that evening, for that day, the assignment is to make sure that the man or woman of God is taken care of.

CHAPTER 7
COVERING UNFAMILIAR LEADER

41

Question: how can an armor bearer get to know a leader well or intimately enough to be able to anticipate what they need, even if it is the first time they meet?

Stay quiet and alert, be discerning, listen, understand the boundaries, be patient, and be in tune with the flow of the Holy Spirit as He leads the man or woman of God - and that's only through the preparation of prayer.

Case in point.

Through the guidance and leadership of Bishop Charles Ross, founder of Judah NOW Church and Kingdom Connection Fellowship, the 2021 Winter Leader Shift Conference was showcased in Baltimore, Maryland.

First assignment: Dr. Torrey Phillips, Founder, Director, and CEO at Faith Factory. Dr. Phillips is an author and renowned speaker who frequents across the nation. Dr. Phillips normally travels alone, and he places his faith in the Lord for everything, even down to believing that the ministry to whom he will let his gift down for the Lord will take care of him.

When I received Dr. Phillips' information, I communicated with him and described what vehicle I was in. In turn, he replied with what he had on. Since Dr. Phillips is used to operating independently, I had to assure him that he does not have to carry the load by himself this time. Without being overbearing yet assertive, I had to create an environment where Dr. Phillips could be comfortable so he could operate freely through the Holy Spirit. Supplying Dr. Phillips with his favorite refreshments helped, although he was appreciative of all that was done for him.

Dr. Phillips' down-to-earth, relaxed demeanor made it easier to serve him as his humidity was purely genuine. When it was time to get Dr. Phillips, we were coordinated and on the same page as if we served together for years. I came up with signals for Dr. Phillips to communicate with me when in need.

Without a miss-step, Dr. Phillips was able to complete his assignment for the Lord and restore God's people.

Next assignment, Dr. Cindy Trimm.

Dr. Trimm is a dynamic, sought-after empowerment author, speaker, thinker, and advocate known across the globe. She has been proclaiming God's Word through her authentic lifestyle for over 30 years. Dr.Trimm is a praying vessel who walks in the authority of Christ and humbly demands respect when she is present.

This situation was unique because Dr. Trimm had her adjutant, Ms. Willis. It was the first time I had to cover an adjutant and the man or woman of God at the same time. Still, the preparation remains the same. Fortunately, I had Ms. Willis' contact information as we were in communication with each other as Dr. Trimm and she was en route to Baltimore.

I was on time, refreshments were provided, and the goosebumps were all over the place. I communicated with Ms. Willis, and inquired about what location number was featured near the baggage claim. Shortly after receiving that information, Dr. Trimm and Ms. Willis walked out, and I escorted them to the vehicle. Dr. Trimm and

Ms. Willis were pleased and I got them to the hotel safely.

When it was time to get Dr. Trimm and Ms. Willis to the conference, I communicated with them with gameplay on how I would assist Ms. Willis so she could serve Dr. Trimm in an unfamiliar place. I did not engage Dr. Trimm and Ms. Willis in any conversation. It is my job to be present yet invisible at the same time. However, the only time I had a conversation with Dr Trimm was when she initiated, but I did not carry on the discussion as I knew Dr. Trimm had to be mentally and spiritually prepared for the people.

As fun-loving, pleasant, and professional as Dr. Trimm is, she was locked in and on a mission.

So, Dr. Trimm and Ms. Willis still wanted to converse. While they were comfortable, I maintained the order of an armor bearer with personality. When we arrived, I started covering Dr. Trimm through Ms. Willis. I escorted Dr. Trimm and Ms. Willis into the church as I carried Ms. Willis' items, while she carried Dr. Trimm's items.

From there, Ms. Willis was on her assignment covering her woman of God while I focused on both of them.

When Dr. Trimm was preaching, I noticed how she was trying to catch her breath. While staying in my place, the first thing that came to mind as I looked at Ms. Willis was, "Are you going to get Dr. Trimm something to drink?"

Ms. Willis sat and watched Dr. Trimm as she continued to cough. Ms. Willis just sat back and was calm and collected without moving a muscle. So, immediately, it came to mind Ms. Willis knew how to handle this situation with Dr. Trimm so I relaxed as the woman of God worked through the coughing. Eventually, Ms. Willis gave Dr. Trimm some water at the appropriate time.

When service was over, and Dr. Trimm, Ms. Willis and I got in the vehicle, we talked about it. Ms. Willis explained that she knew not to give anything to Dr. Trimm. Dr. Trimm explained as she recognized over the years of teaching, that it is always different types of wind that go into her mouth, and she has to control it. Plus, when she drinks, especially water, that's like her 'Monster,' her power energy drink. So, Ms. Willis knows that by getting the woman of God something to drink, water, Dr. Trimm would preach for another hour, which Dr. Trimm expressed with laughter.

That is the reason why I did not see Dr. Trimm's adjutant jump up to give her something to drink because Dr. Trimm does not want anything. "This is something I have to exercise myself through (coughing) while I'm up there, and (Ms. Willis) allows me to work my way through," said Dr. Trimm. Further into the message, when Ms. Willis witnessed how the airflow went into Dr. Trimm's air pocket, that's when her adjutant jumped up to give Dr. Trimm something as they were on the same page, in one accord.

As an adjutant, one has to learn and listen without always being told what the man or woman of God needs. Clearly, Ms. Willis has been covering Dr. Trimm for a lengthy time period to know the airflow Dr. Trimm was breathing in order to know the appropriate time to interject with assistance. It takes time and different situations to understand how to be effective for the man or woman of God.

Without question, the overlooked responsibilities mentioned of having the *Heart To Serve, Being In Place, Preparedness, Looking The Part, and Being The Part* were effective in covering the unfamiliar leaders. Notwithstanding, being *prepared financially* was a necessary added bonus, and the necessity of this responsibility was on display.

As was mentioned earlier about being prepared financially, the necessity of this qualification surfaced when I was assigned to the leaders of the Winter Conference. After Dr. Trimm completed her assignment, which was late in the evening, her adjutant and she wanted something to eat. Restaurants normally start to shut down at 11 pm. Choices were extremely limited. However, it was still my responsibility to feed Dr. Trimm and Ms. Willis. This is when an armor bearer must be strategic financially because situations surface often, especially when a special guest has to be covered.

After driving around Baltimore City and finding out what they had taste for, I took them to a spot and Dr. Trimm and her adjutant ordered a lot of food. The best part, Dr. Trimm and her adjutant enjoyed everything. This mighty woman of God who is world renowned is one of the greatest individuals I have ever met, and it was not just an honor to cover her, but it was an absolute pleasure.

For Dr. Phillips, it was the same situation. He needed something to eat and it was late. Now, Dr. Phillips is a snacker (I love it)! He asked me what I liked about the restaurant I presented to him. I informed him, ordered and got it for Dr. Phillips. He was a happy man, but there was one thing missing: chips! "I got to have my chips," Dr. Phillips stated.

We stopped at two places because one of those places was surprisingly closed. Nevertheless, I made sure Dr. Phillips was all set. After getting Dr. Trimm and Dr. Phillips to their respective places of rest, when it was time to pick them up early the next morning, refreshments were provided. The humility of these two godly individuals is amazing.

Now, could these leaders pay for their own food? Absolutely, because they are blessed with wealth through their obedience to the Lord. They did not need anything from me. Still, they were my responsibility, my assignment and they needed to know comfort in a strange land. Dr. Trimm, her adjutant, Ms. Willis, and Dr. Phillips were extremely grateful.

These are a few examples of why an armor bearer has to be prepared financially to operate in this capacity to handle any circumstance, just in case the ministry does not account for it. Situations will come up, and the armor bearer has to be prepared for it.

Preparation was paramount. Not only due to my assignment, but because I'm a reflection of Jesus Christ. Decency, order and excellence is what God demands for His mouth pieces and it is the armor bearer's duty to provide what is required, without expecting anything in return.

CHAPTER 8
NOT FOR YOU

Apparently, there is a self-evaluation an individual has to check for within themselves long before accepting the assignment of being an armor bearer. Are you willing to suffer physically if something was to happen? Are you willing to take a bullet for the man or woman of God? If not, this walk is not for you. People are potentially anything without Christ, meaning that individuals who are not following Christ are unstable. This situation has to be considered.

We learned that if an individual is not trustworthy and can not hold personal information shared with them, this walk is not for you. Exposing or uncovering the man or woman of God is, frankly, ungodly, and there is no place for you to serve a leader.

Can you attend service without being a part of the service? If you feel that you can not help yourself during praise and worship and not get caught in the spirit or emotions, this walk is not for you.

This walk demands your full attention to be on the man or woman of God at all times. As mentioned, you need to have been in the Lord's presence prior to being with the man or woman of God or already be in the spirit of worship so you can be properly in place for your leader.

Are you afraid to offend people if they cross the line? If so, this walk is not for you.

Sometimes, you may have to tell someone, 'Not today. Not today.' Sometimes, you may have to urge the man or woman of God to move quickly because you have to get them away from the people. There will be situations where you may have to be the bad guy because the man or woman of God may not want to talk after service because they are tired.

You will have to be the one to orchestrate the man or woman of God's exit for their safety. You will have to be willing to take the hit for the man or woman of God, allowing individuals to be upset with you instead of the man or woman of God to keep peace for them.

UNTIL NEXT TIME

On the surface, being an armor bearer appears to be a glorified position in Christ. Some get to travel the world, all expenses paid. The adjutant has the privilege to stand alongside the man or woman of God in front of hundreds of people and get to know them in ways saints would dream of.

Now, without the expectations, accountabilities, and responsibilities mentioned throughout this teaching, many probably would realize that being armor bearer is not what it appears to be. Many readers may say, 'Does it take all of this?' The answer is yes, and then some (keep up with the series).

When it is understood that the walk of an armor bearer is not just a Sunday morning or a preaching engagement with the man or woman of God, but it is a demanding lifestyle with many obstacles to juggle. It is only a burden if the proper expectations are not met, accountabilities are not accounted for, and the responsibilities are taken with importance.

When these foundational principles are exercised with the right attitude, heart, and passion, then you will have Integrity for the Mission.